NICK JOINS IN

WRITTEN and ILLUSTRATED by JOE LASKER

Albert Whitman & Company, *Chicago*

To
CAROLINE

Library of Congress Cataloging in Publication Data

Lasker, Joe.
    Nick joins in.

    (A Concept book)
    SUMMARY: When Nick, confined to a wheelchair,
enters a regular classroom for the first time as a result
of U.S. Public Law 94-142, he and his new classmates must
resolve their initial apprehensions about mainstreaming.
    [1. Physically handicapped—Fiction. 2. School stories.
3. Mainstreaming in education—Fiction] I. Title.
PZ7.L327Ni   [E]   79-29637
    ISBN 0-8075-5612-2

*A free appropriate public education must be
guaranteed for all handicapped children.
Whenever possible, handicapped children will be
educated alongside non-handicapped children,
a practice known as "mainstreaming."*
                    U.S. Public Law 94-142

Nick was scared.

He didn't know what to expect.

Soon he would be going to school instead of school coming to him. No longer would a teacher visit his home.

Nick's mother had told him, "You'll be going to school, the way other children do. You won't be so lonely anymore. Before you start, we'll visit your school. We'll meet your new teacher and her aide."

Nick, who couldn't walk or run, was worried. "How will I go up and down the stairs?" he asked himself. "Will I be as smart as the other children? Will they want to play with me?"

Nick talked to his parents.

"How can I go to school in my wheelchair?" he asked.
"What if the kids don't like me? Will there be anyone else
who can't walk?"

His mother said, "Nick, at first the other children
will stare at you and ask questions. You'll all feel
a little strange with each other."

"But after a while you'll get used to each other and be friends," his father said.

On and on, Nick's questions tumbled out. His parents grew tired of them. But they knew this was Nick's way of getting ready for school.

"We understand why you feel so worried," they said.

Nick felt a little better.

Meanwhile, the school was getting ready for Nick.
Over the steps, workers built a ramp for his wheelchair.

A special desk was brought into Mrs. Becker's classroom.
She told her children that the desk would be used by
a new boy. She told them about Nick and his wheelchair.

"Will the new boy like us?" asked Timmie.

"Will we catch what he has?" asked Nina.

"No, it's not catching," Mrs. Becker said.

On Wednesday morning a small yellow bus
carried Nick to his school.

A teacher's aide met the bus.

"We hope you like our school, Nick," she said.

Then the aide pushed him up the new ramp, through big doors, and into a long hallway.

Inside the school, children rushed everywhere.
Never before had Nick been among so many boys and
girls. A bell clanged loudly. It frightened him.
The children all disappeared into their classrooms.

Many doors faced the hallway. If he were ever alone,
Nick thought, how would he find the right door?
He looked for things to help him remember where to go.
    The aide wheeled Nick through one door,
and he knew he was in his classroom.

veryone in the room looked at Nick.
Mrs. Becker smiled at him.
"We're glad you're here," she said.
Then she introduced him to the boys and girls.
Nick wondered if he'd ever remember all their names.
He stared at the floor, wishing he were back home.

No one spoke. Then Mrs. Becker said, "Nick, I
think the children would like to ask you some
questions. Is that all right?"

Nick nodded, still looking down.

Slowly his classmates gathered around.

Rachel asked the first question. "Why do you
have to use a wheelchair?"

"Because I can't walk," Nick said, not looking at her.

"Why can't you walk?" asked Nina.

"Because my legs don't grow right."

"Why is that?" asked Timmie.

Nick looked at him. "I was born that way."

Cindy pointed to the braces on Nick's legs.
"Why do you wear those?" she said.

"They help me stand," Nick told her.

When Mrs. Becker thought the children had satisfied
enough of their curiosity, she said, "All right, boys
and girls, it's time to begin our work."

She helped Nick get settled. Then it was his turn
to look around and satisfy his curiosity.

Nick looked at all the children. He looked at
his teacher and at the bright pictures on the walls.
He looked around for a long time.

He didn't feel so scared anymore.

He decided he might like school.

Days went by.
Nick and the other children grew used to each other.
They learned from one another.

Without being asked, people helped Nick.
Nick helped people, too. Sometimes he helped
the gym teacher open windows with the long window pole.

Nick made friends. One of them was Timmie.

Timmie needed special help, too—not from other children, but from his teachers.

Nick loved recess. For the first time in his life
he played outdoor games with children. He couldn't
run like Timmie, but he moved fast.

What Nick wished for most was to play ball like
the others. How fast and high they jumped and darted!
To Nick, that was like flying.

One afternoon there was a ball game. Higher and
higher the ball went, until it landed on the roof of the gym.
   The ball rolled to the edge of the roof, but instead
of dropping down, it stuck in the rain gutter.
   All the children groaned.

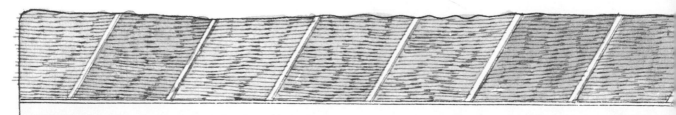

Timmie threw a basketball to jar the ball out
of the gutter. But the ball didn't move.

Nina threw a stone, but that didn't help.

A teacher lifted Ben onto his shoulders, but Ben still
couldn't reach high enough.

"Oh, we'll never finish our game," complained Timmie.

Nick had an idea. He wheeled away from the playground.

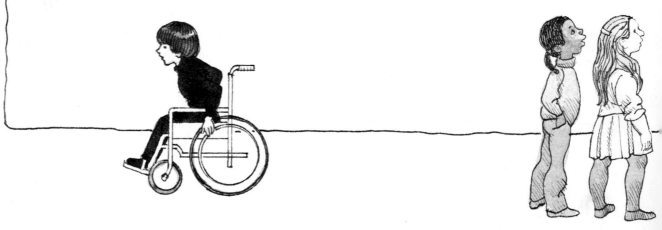

He rode through the open gym door, past the tall
gym windows, straight to the corner where the window
pole was. He took the pole and wheeled back outside.

The children looked helplessly at the stuck ball.
Everyone had given up.

Nina saw Nick coming. "Nick to the rescue,"
she shouted. "In the nick of time!"

"Excuse me, please," said Nick, wheeling through
the crowd. He held the slim pole tightly. No one
was going to take it from him.

He stopped under the gutter and looked up. He raised
the pole and poked the ball loose. Down it dropped.
"Hooray for Nick!" everybody cheered.

Nick felt he was flying.